How To Make Rug

How To Make Rugs

by Candace Wheeler

Copyright © 10/1/2015
Jefferson Publication

ISBN-13: 978-1517622831

Printed in the United States of America

All rights reserved. No part of this book may be reprinted or reproduced or utilized in any form or by any electronic, mechanical, or other means, now known or hereafter invented, including photocopying and recording, or in any form of storage or retrieval system, without prior permission in writing from the publisher.'

Table of Contents

FOREWORD. 3
   HOME INDUSTRIES AND DOMESTIC MANUFACTURES. 3
CHAPTER I. 10
   RUG WEAVING. 10
CHAPTER II. 16
   THE PATTERN. 16
CHAPTER III. 21
   DYEING. 21
CHAPTER IV. 26
   INGRAIN CARPET RUGS. 26
CHAPTER V. 29
   WOVEN RAG PORTIERES. 29
CHAPTER VI. 35
   WOOLEN RUGS. 35
CHAPTER VII. 44
   COTTON RUGS. 44
CHAPTER VIII. 51
   LINSEY WOOLSEY. 51
NEIGHBOURHOOD INDUSTRIES 57
   AFTER-WORD 57

FOREWORD.

HOME INDUSTRIES AND DOMESTIC MANUFACTURES.

The subject of Home Industries is beginning to attract the attention of those who are interested in political economy and the general welfare of the country, and thoughtful people are asking themselves why, in all the length and breadth of America, there are no well-established and prosperous domestic manufactures.

We have no articles of use or luxury made in *homes* which are objects of commercial interchange or sources of family profit. To this general statement there are but few exceptions, and curiously enough these are, for the most part, in the work of our native Indians.

A stranger in America, wishing—after the manner of travelers—to carry back something characteristic of the country, generally buys what we call "Indian curiosities"—moccasins, baskets, feather-work, and the one admirable and well-established product of Indian manufacture, the Navajo blanket. But these hardly represent the mass of our people.

We may add to the list of Indian industries, lace making, which is being successfully taught at some of the reservations, but as it is not as yet even a self-supporting industry, the above-named "curiosities" and the Navajo blanket stand alone as characteristic hand-work produced by native races; while from our own, or that of the co-existent Afro-American, we have nothing to show in the way of true domestic manufactures.

When we contrast this want of production with the immense home product of Europe, Asia, parts of Africa, and South America—and even certain islands of the Southern Seas—we cannot help feeling a sort of dismay at the contrast; and it is only by a careful study of the conditions which have made the difference that we become reassured. It is, in fact, our very prosperity, the exceptionally favourable circumstances which are a part of farming life in this country, which has hitherto diverted efforts into other channels.

These conditions did not exist during the early days of America, and we know that while there was little commercial exchange of home commodities, many of the arts which are used to such profitable purpose abroad existed in this country and served greatly to modify home expenses and increase home comforts. To account for the cessation of these household industries, it is only necessary to notice the drift of certain periods in the short history of America's settlement and development.

We shall see that the decline of domestic manufactures in New England and the Middle States was coincident with two rapidly increasing movements, one of which was the opening and settlement of the great West, and the other the establishment of cotton and woolen mills throughout the country.

In short, the abundant acreage of Western lands, fertile beyond the dreams of New England or Old World tillers, threw the entire business of production or family support upon the man. The profit of his easily acquired farm land was so great and certain that it became almost a reproach to him to have his womenkind busy themselves with other than necessary household duties.

The cotton and woolen mills stood ready to supply the needed material for clothing, and it was positive economy to push the spinning-wheel out of sight under the garret eaves and chop up the bulky loom for firewood. The wife and daughters might reputably cook and clean for the men whose business it was to cover the black acres with golden wheat, but spinning and weaving were decidedly unfashionable occupations. Even the emigrants from countries where the spinning and weaving habit was an inheritance as well as a necessity, were governed by the custom of the country, and devoted the entire energy of the family to the raising of crops.

It is, in fact, owing to fortunate circumstances that, if we except the mountain regions of the South, there are no longer farmhouse or domestic manufactures in America.

This, as I have said, only goes to prove the hitherto unexampled prosperity of the country. In fact, the absence of these very industries means that there are greater sources of profit within the reach of farming households.

This being so, it is natural to ask, why the re-establishment of farmhouse manufactures, or the encouragement and development of them, is a desirable movement.

There are exceedingly good individual and personal reasons; and there are also commercial and national ones, which should not be ignored.

All farmers are not successful. There are many poor as well as rich ones; and the wife of a poor farmer has less pecuniary independence, less money to spend, and fewer ways of gaining it, than any other woman of equal education and character in America.

A poor farmer is often obliged to pay out for labour, fencing, stock, insurance and taxes every dollar gained by the sale of his crops, and if by good luck or good management there should be a small excess, he is apt to hoard it against unlooked-for emergencies. This, at first enforced economy, grows to be the habit of his life, so that even if he becomes well-to-do, or even rich, he distrusts exceedingly the wisdom of any expenditure save his own.

A mechanic, or a man in any small line of business, must trust his wife with the disbursement of a certain part of the family income. It passes through her hands in the way of housekeeping, and the management of it exercises and develops her faculties; but the wife of the farmer has no such interest. The farm is expected to supply the family living, and this blessed fact becomes almost a curse when it deprives the wife of the mental stimulus incident to the management of resources.

Added to this there is often, at least through the winter, partial or complete isolation from neighbourly or public interests. The great crops of the country are produced under circumstances which necessitate distance from even the most limited social centres, and that the farmer's wife suffers from this we know, not only from observation, but from the statistics of insane asylums. And here I am tempted to quote from a letter of a close student of farmhouse life in the West. She writes:

"That the farmer himself, as isolated and hard worked, makes no such record, I believe due to the mental tonic, the broadening influence that comes from a sense of responsibility in life's larger affairs. The woman works like a machine, irresponsible as to final results; the man like a thinking, planning, responsible, independent human being."

This seems to me a very fair statement of the case. The woman, who misses social companionship, and who has not the saving influence of administration and responsibility even in her own household, is narrowed to a very small point in life's affairs, and it is inevitable that she should suffer from it. The variety of her work also has dwindled. Cooking and house-cleaning follow each other in monotonous routine, with too much of it at planting and harvest seasons and too little at others. She has not even the pleasure of comparison and emulation in her daily work; it neither exercises her faculties nor stimulates her thought.

During the winter months she has abundant leisure for a harvest of her own, in some interesting manufacture adapted to her education and circumstances, and in the prosecution of these she would be brought into a bond of common interest with other women. So far I have spoken only of the individual and personal reasons for which certain domestic and artistic industries well might be encouraged; but the public and economic reasons are easy to find.

In looking at the variety and bulk of our national imports, we may be surprised to see how large a proportion of them are of domestic origin. In fact, nearly everything which comes under the head of artistic products is the result of domestic industry. The beauty and simplicity of many of these things is surprising, and yet they have required neither unusual talent or careful training. They are simply the result of the *habit* of production, and their value is in the personal expression we find in them. They have always this advantage over mechanical manufacture, and can be safely relied upon to find a market in the face of close mechanical imitation.

Among these domestic products we shall find the laces of all countries, Ireland, Belgium, France, Italy, Sweden and Russia contributing this beautiful manufacture, from finest to coarsest quality. It is as common a process as knitting in the homes of many countries, and the fact of it being successfully taught in the Indian cabins of the far West proves that it is not a difficult accomplishment. Embroideries, in all countries but our own, are common and profitable home productions; and when we come to hand-weavings the variety is infinite. In practical England, the value of hand-weavings in linens has led to the introduction of small "parlour looms" from Sweden; and damasks of special designs are woven for special customers who appreciate their charm and worth.

Of all hand processes, weaving is the most generally or widely applicable, and the range of beautiful production possible to the simplest weaving is almost beyond calculation.

Many of the costly Eastern rugs are as simply woven as a Navajo blanket, or even a rag carpet. The process is in many cases almost identical, the variation being only in closeness or fineness of warp and arrangement of colour.

I have been much interested of late in an application of art to a local industry in New Hampshire. It is one which seems to prevail to a greater or less degree all through New England, and the product is called "pulled rugs." The process consists of drawing finely cut rags through some loose, strong cloth, mainly bagging or burlap. I have seen these rugs at Bar Harbor and along the Massachusetts coast for many years, and while they possessed the merit of durability, they were, for the most part, so ugly and unattractive that only the most sympathetic personal interest in the maker would induce one to purchase them. The change that has been wrought in this manufacture by an intelligent application of art is really marvelous. The product came under the attention of a woman trained in that valuable school, "The Institute of Artist Artisans." She tried the experiment of using new material carefully dyed to follow certain Oriental designs, and the result is a smooth, velvety, thick-piled rug, which cannot be distinguished from a fine Oriental rug of the same pattern. The cost of this manufacture is necessarily considerable, since the process is slow and the material costly. But in spite of these disadvantages, the drawn rugs have met with deserved favour, and are a source of profitable labour to the community. It is undoubtedly the beginning of an important industry, which owes its success entirely to the art education of one woman.

There is an improvement somewhat akin to this in the weaving of rag-carpet rugs, and this is not confined to one locality. It consists in the use of *new* rags, carefully selected as to colour both of rags and warp, and the result is surprisingly good.

One might say that we have in this country peculiar advantages for positive artistic excellence as well as volume of production. We grow our own wool and cotton. We have a great and growing population, with such application of mechanical invention to routine and necessary work as greatly to reduce household labour. Added to this, there has been during the last ten years so much and such general art study as to have created a sort of diffused love of art manufactures, so that many of the people who would naturally adopt the work would have an instructive judgment regarding it. I should not be afraid to predict great and even peculiar excellence in any domestic manufacture which became the habit of any given locality.

The subject of our domestic industries is one which should fall naturally within the objects of women's clubs. If every woman's club in the country chose from its members those who by artistic instinct or education, and the possession of practical ability, were fitted to lead in the work, and made of them a committee on home industries, the reports from it would soon become a matter of absorbing interest to the club, and the productions made under the protection, so to speak, of the club, would have an advantage that any commercial business would consider invaluable. Neither would the advantage be limited by the interest of a single club. That great social engine, "The Federation of Women's Clubs," can wield an almost magical power in the creation of interests or encouragement of effort, and the federation of organizations, each one exchanging experiences as well as products, would be an ideal means of growth and extension.

The machinery for the work exists in almost every county of every State of the Union, and with the threefold interest of the promotion of practical art, that of increased manufacture, and the extension of that sisterhood which is one of the most Christian-like and desirable aims of women's clubs, it would seem a natural and congenial effort.

The best results of this general awakening will probably be in the South. Certainly no conditions could be more favourable than those existing in the Cumberland Mountains, where wool and cotton grown upon the rough farms are habitually spun and woven and dyed in the home cabin. The dyes are often made from walnut bark, pokeberry, and certain nuts and roots which have been found capable of "fast" stain and are easily procured. Unfortunately, the facility with which aniline dyes can be used is not unknown. The "linsey woolsey," which is not only a common manufacture in the farmhouses, but the common wear of both men and women, is an interesting and good manufacture, capable of much wider use than it enjoys at present.

And linsey woolsey is not the only home weaving done in the Cumberland Mountains. The showing of cotton homespun towel weaving at the Atlanta Exposition was a feature of the Exposition, and the homespun blankets of the various kinds which one finds in common use are only a step removed from the process of the admirable Navajo blanket.

We see from these different possibilities and indications, that although we are still a people without true home productions, there is every reason to believe that this condition will not be a lasting one, and that before many years we shall find the special advantages and general cultivation of the country have not only produced but given character to a large domestic manufacture.

CHAPTER I.

RUG WEAVING.

Rag carpets have been made and used in farmhouses for many generations, but it is only of late that there has been a general demand in all country houses for home-made piazza rugs, bedroom rugs, and rugs for general use.

It has been found that the best and most durable rugs for these purposes, and for bath-rooms for town and city houses, can be made of cotton or woolen rags sewed and woven in the regular old-fashioned rag-carpet way, the difference being—and it is rather a large difference—that the rags must be new instead of old, and that the colors must be good and carefully chosen instead of being used indiscriminately, and in addition to this it must be woven in two-yard lengths, with a border and fringe at either end. This being done, good, attractive and salable rugs can be made of almost any color, and suitable for many purposes. It is an industry perfectly adapted to farmhouse conditions, and if well followed out would make a regular income for the women of the family.

The cumbrous old wooden loom is still doing a certain amount of work in nearly every country neighbourhood, and it is capable of a greatly enlarged and much more profitable practice. I find very little if any difference in the rugs woven upon these and the modern steel loom. It is true that the work is lighter and weaving goes faster upon the latter, and where a person or family makes an occupation of weaving it is probably better to have the latest improvements; but it is possible to begin and to make a success of rag rug weaving upon an old-fashioned loom, and as a rule old-fashioned weavers have little to learn in new methods.

This small book is intended as a help in adapting their work to modern demands, as well as to open a new field to the farmer's family during the winter months, when their time is not necessarily occupied with growing and securing crops.

WEAVING

It does not undertake to teach any one who buys or has inherited a loom to begin weaving without any further preparation. The warping or threading of it must be *seen* to be understood, but when that is once learned, all of the rest is a matter of practice and experiment, and is really no more difficult than any other domestic art. One would not expect to spin without being shown how to pull the wool and turn the wheel at the same time, or even to sew or knit without some sort of instruction, and the same is true of weaving.

There are many old looms still to be found in the garrets of farmhouses, and where one has been inherited it is best to begin learning to weave upon it instead of substituting a new one, since the same knowledge answers for both. Probably some older member of the family, or at least some old neighbour, will be able to teach the new beginner how to set up the loom and to proceed from that to actual weaving. After this is learned it rests with one's self to become a good weaver, a practical dyer, and to put colors together which are both harmonious and effective.

What I have chiefly tried to show is how to get proper materials and how to use them to the best advantage. I think it is safe to say that no domestic art is capable of such important results from a pecuniary point of view, or so important an extension in the direction of practical art. Where it is used as an art-process and an interesting occupation, by women of leisure, it is capable of the finest results, and there is no reason why these results should not become a matter of business profit.

Rag carpets have generally been woven of rags cut from any old garments cast aside by the household—coats and trousers too old for patching, sheets and pillow-cases too tender to use, calico, serge, bits of woolen stuffs old and new, went into the carpet basket, to be cut or torn into strips, sewed indiscriminately together, and rolled into balls until there should be enough of them for the work of the loom. When this time came the loom would be warped with white cotton or purple yarn, dyed with "sugar paper" or logwood, and the carpet woven. Even with this entire carelessness as to any other result than that of a useful floor covering, the rag carpet, with its "hit or miss" mixture, was not a bad thing; and a very small degree of attention has served to give it a respectable place in domestic manufactures. But it is capable of being carried much farther; in fact, I know of no process which can so easily be made to produce really good and beautiful results as rag carpet weaving.

The first material needed is what are called carpet warps, and these can be purchased in different weights and sizes and more or less reliable colours in every country store, this fact alone showing the prevalence of home weaving, since the yarns are not—at least to my knowledge—used for any other purpose.

The cost of warp, dyed or undyed, depends upon the quantity required, or, in other words, upon its being purchased at wholesale or retail. At retail it costs twenty cents per pound, and at wholesale sixteen. To buy of a wholesale dealer one must be able to order at least a hundred pounds, and as this would weave but a hundred and fifty rugs it would not be too large a quantity to have on hand for even a moderate amount of weaving. These prices refer only to ordinary cotton warps, and not to fine "silk finish," to linen, or even to silk ones, each of which has its special use and price.

In all of them fast colour is a most desirable quality, and, indeed, for truly good work a necessity. I have found but two of the colours which are upon ordinary sale to be reasonably fast, and those are a very deep red and the ordinary orange. The latter will run when dipped in water; in fact, it will give out dye to such good purpose that I have sometimes used the water in which it has been steeped to dye cotton rags, as it gives a very good and quite fast lemon yellow.

It follows, then, that in weaving rugs (which must be washable) with orange warp, the warp must be steeped in warm water before using. It can be used in that state, or it can be *set* with alum, or it can be dipped in a thin indigo dye and made into a good and fast green.

The only recourse of the domestic weaver who wishes to establish her rugs as of the very best make is to dye her own warps; and this is not only an easy but a most interesting process; so much so, in fact, that I am tempted to enlarge upon it as a practical study for the young people of the family. It is necessary at the very beginning to put much stress upon the value of fast colour in the warping yarn, since a faded warp will entirely neutralize the colour of the rags, and spoil the beauty of the most successful rug.

The most necessary and widely applicable colour needed in warps, or, indeed, in rags, is a perfectly fast blue in different depths, and this can only be secured by indigo. Aniline blue in cotton is never sun-fast and rarely will stand washing, but a good indigo blue will neither run or fade, and is therefore precisely what is needed for domestic manufacture. Fortunately, the dye-tub has been, in the past at least, a close companion of the loom, and most old-fashioned farmers' wives know how to use it. With this one can command reliable blue warps of all shades; and when we come to directions for making washable rugs its importance will be seen.

As I have said, by dipping orange warp in medium indigo blue a fast and vivid green can be secured, and these two tints, together with orange and red, give as many colours as one needs for rug weaving; they give, in fact, a choice of five colours—orange, red, blue, green and white. Orange and red are both colours which can be relied upon when prepared from the ordinary "Magic" dyes of commerce. Turkey red especially is safe to last, even when applied to cotton. In the general disapproval of mineral dyes, this one may certainly be excepted, as well as the crimson red known as "cardinal," which is both durable and beautiful, in silk or woolen fibre or texture.

After good warps are secured, the second material needed is *filling*; and here the subject of old and new rags is to be considered. Of course, cloth which has served other purposes, as in sheets, pillow-cases, curtains, dress skirts, etc., is still capable of prolonged wear when the thin parts are removed and those which are fairly strong are folded and bunched into carpet filling; and for family use, or limited sale, such rags—dyed in some colour—are really desirable. Good varieties of washable rugs can be made of half-worn cotton without dyeing (although they will not be as durable as if made from unworn muslin) by using blue warps to white fillings. The colour effects and methods of weaving will be the same whether old or new rags are used; but in making a study of rag rug weaving from the point of view of building up an important industry, it is necessary to consider only the use of new rags and how to procure the best of them at the cheapest rates.

There is a certain amount of what is called waste in all cloth mills, either cotton, wool or silk, and also in the manufacture of every kind of clothing. The waste from cotton mills, consisting for the most part of "piece ends," imperfect beginnings or endings, which must be torn off when the piece is made up, are exactly suitable for carpet weaving; and, in fact, if made for the purpose could hardly be better. These can be bought for from ten to twelve cents per pound. The same price holds for ginghams and for coloured cottons of various sorts.

Cutting from shirt-making and clothing establishments are not as good. In shirt cuttings the cloth varies a good deal in thickness, and, in addition to this disadvantage, cannot be torn into strips, many of the pieces being bias, and therefore having to be cut. It is true that while this entails additional use of time in preparation, bias rags are a more elastic filling than straight ones, and if uniformly and carefully cut and sewed a rug made from them is worth more and will probably sell for more than one made of straight rags.

Shirt cuttings sell for about three cents per pound, and while a proportion of them are too small for use and would have to be re-sold for paper rags, the cost of material for cotton rugs would still be very trifling. Suitable woolen rags from the mills sell for twenty-five cents per pound. Tailors' and dressmakers' cuttings are much cheaper, and very advantageous arrangements can be made with large establishments if one is prepared to take all they have to offer.

One difficulty with woolen rags from tailoring establishments is in the sombreness of the colours; but much can be done by judicious sorting and sewing of the rags, for it is astonishing how bits of every conceivable colour will melt together when brought into a mixed mass; also if they are woven upon a red warp the effect is brightened.

Having secured materials of different kinds, the next step is in the cutting and sewing, and here also new methods must step in.

The old-fashioned way of sewing carpet rags—that is, simply *tacking* them together with a large needle and coarse thread—will not answer at all in this new development of rug making. The filling must be smooth, without lumps or rag ends, and the joinings absolutely fast and fairly inconspicuous. Some of the new rags from cotton or woolen mills come in pieces from a quarter to a half-yard in length and the usual width of the cloth. These can be sewed together on the sewing machine, lapping and basting them before sewing. They should lap from a quarter to a half inch and have two sewings, one at either edge of the lap. If sewed in this way they can afterward be torn into strips, using the scissors to cut across seams. It can be performed very speedily when one is accustomed to it, and is absolutely secure, so that no rag ends can ever be seen in the finished weaving.

If the cloth pieces which are to be used for rags are not wide enough to sew on the sewing machine, they should be lapped and sewed by hand in the same way, unless they happen to have selvedge ends, in which case they should by all means be strongly overhanded. This makes the best possible joining, as it is no thicker than the rest of the rag filling, and consequently gives an even surface. Good sewing is the first step toward making good and workmanlike rugs.

Whenever the rags can be torn instead of cut, it is preferable, as it secures uniform width. The width, of course, must vary according to the quality of cloth and weight desired in the rug. A certain weight is necessary to make it lie smoothly, as a light rug will not stay in place on the floor. In ordinary cotton cloth an inch wide strip is not too heavy and will pinch into the required space. If, however, a door-hanging or lounge-cover is being woven, the rags may be made half that width.

CHAPTER II.

THE PATTERN.

When proper warp and filling are secured, experimental weaving may begin. If the loom is an old-fashioned wooden one, it will weave only in yard widths, and this yard width takes four hundred and fifty threads of warp. Warping the loom is really the only difficult or troublesome part of plain weaving, and therefore it is best to put in as long a warp as one is likely to use in one colour. One and a half pounds of cotton rags will make one yard of weaving.

The simplest trial will be the weaving of white filling, either old or new, with a warp of medium indigo blue. Of course each warp must be long enough to weave several rugs; and the first one, to make the experiment as simple as possible, should be of white rags alone upon a blue warp. There must be an allowance of five inches of warp for fringe before the weaving is begun, and ten inches at the end of the rug to make a fringe for both first and second rugs. Sometimes the warp is set in groups of three, with a corresponding interval between, and this—if the tension is firm and the rags soft—gives a sort of honeycomb effect which is very good.

The grouping of the warp is especially desirable in one-coloured rugs, as it gives a variation of surface which is really attractive.

When woven, the rug should measure three feet by six, without the fringe. This is to be knotted, allowing six threads to a knot. This kind of bath-rug—which is the simplest thing possible in weaving—will be found to be truly valuable, both for use and effect. If the filling is sufficiently heavy, and especially if it is made of half-worn rags, it will be soft to the feet, and can be as easily washed as a white counterpane; in fact, it can be thrown on the grass in a heavy shower and allowed to wash and bleach itself.

Several variations can be made upon this blue warp in the way of borders and color-splashes by using any indigo-dyed material mixed with the white rags. Cheap blue ginghams, "domestics" or half-worn and somewhat faded blue denims will be of the right depth of color, but as a rule new denim is of too dark a blue to introduce with pure white filling.

The illustration called "The Onteora Rug" is made by using a proportion of a half-pound of blue rags to the two and a half of white required to make up the three pounds of cotton filling required in a six-foot rug. This half-pound of blue should be distributed through the rug in three portions, and the two and a half pounds of white also into three, so as to insure an equal share of blue to every third of the rug. After this division is made it is quite immaterial how it goes together. The blue rags may be long, short or medium, and the effect is almost certain to be equally good.

The side border in "The Lois Rug," which is made upon the same blue warp, is separately woven, and afterward added to the plain white rug with blue ends, but an irregular side border can easily be made by sewing the rags in lengths of a half-yard, alternating the blue and white, and keeping the white rags in the centre of the rug while weaving.

These three or four variations of style in what we may call washable rugs are almost equally good where red warp is used, substituting Turkey red rags with the white filling instead of blue. An orange warp can be used for an orange and white rug, mixing the white filling with ordinary orange cotton cloth.

The effect may be reversed by using a white warp with a red, blue or yellow filling, making the borders and splashes with white. One of the best experiments in plain weaving I have seen is a red rug of the "Lois" style, using white warp and mixed white and green gingham rags for the borders, while the body of the rug is in shaded red rags.

This, however, brings us to the question of color in fillings, which must be treated separately.

THE ONTEORA RUG

Of course, variations of all kinds can be made in washable rugs. Light and dark blue rags can be used in large proportion with white ones to make a "hit or miss," and where a darker rug is considered better for household use it can be made entirely of dark and light blue on a white warp; the same thing can be done in reds, yellows and greens. Brown can be used with good effect mixed with orange, using orange warp; or orange, green and brown will make a good combination on a white warp. In almost every variety of rug except where blue warp is used a red stripe in the border will be found an improvement.

A very close, evenly distributed red warp, with white filling, will make a pink rug good enough and pretty enough for the daintiest bedroom. If it is begun and finished with a half-inch of the same warp used as filling, it makes a sort of border; and this, with the red fringe, completes what every one will acknowledge is an exceptionally good piece of floor furnishing.

In using woolen rags, which are apt to be much darker in colour than cotton, a white, red or yellow warp is more apt to be effective than either a green or a blue; in fact, it is quite safe to say that light filling should go with dark warp and dark filling with light or white.

There is an extremely good style of rag rug made at Isle Lamotte, in Vermont, where very dark blue or green woolen rags are woven upon a white warp, with a design of arrows in white at regular intervals at the sides. This design is made by turning back the filling at a given point and introducing a piece of white filling, which in turn is turned back when the length needed for the design is woven and another dark one introduced, each one to be turned back at the necessary place and taken up in the next row. Of course, while the design is in progress one must use several pieces of filling in each row of weaving.

The black border can only be made by introducing a large number of short pieces of the contrasting colour which is to be used in the design and tacking them in place as the weaving proceeds. Of course, in this case thin cloth should be used for the colour-blocks, as otherwise the doubling of texture would make an uneven surface. If the rug is a woolen one, not liable to be washed, this variation of color in pattern can be cleverly made by brushing the applied color pieces lightly with *glue*. Of course, in this case the design will show only on the upper side of the rug. In fact, the only way to make the design show equally on both sides is by turning back the warp, as in the arrow design, or by actually cutting out and sewing in pieces of colour.

By following out the device of using glue for fastening the bits of colour which make border designs many new and very interesting effects can be obtained, as most block and angle forms can be produced by lines made in weaving. It is only where the rug must be constantly subject to washing that they are not desirable. It must be remembered that the warp threads bind them into place, after they are glue-fastened.

Large rugs for centres of rooms can be made of woolen rags by weaving a separate narrow border for the two sides. If the first piece is three feet wide by eight in length, and a foot-wide border is added at the sides, it will make a rug five feet wide by eight feet long; or if two eight-foot lengths are sewn together, with a foot-wide border, it will make an eight-by-eight centre rug. The border should be of black or very dark coloured filling. In making a bordered rug, two dark ends must be woven on the central length of the rug—that is, one foot of black or dark rags can be woven on each end and six feet of the "hit or miss" effect in the middle. This gives a strip of eight feet long, including two dark ends. The separate narrow width, one foot wide and sixteen feet in length, must be added to this, eight feet on either side. The border must be very strongly sewn in order to give the same strength as in the rest of the rug.

The same plan can be carried out in larger rugs, by sewing breadths together and adding a border, but they are not easily lifted, and are apt to pull apart by their own weight. Still, the fact remains that very excellent and handsome rugs can be made from rags, in any size required to cover the floor of a room, by sewing the breadths and adding borders, and if care and taste are used in the combinations as good an effect can be secured as in a much more costly flooring.

The ultimate success of all these different methods of weaving rag rugs depends upon the amount of beauty that can be put into them. They possess all the necessary qualities of durability, usefulness and inexpensiveness, but if they cannot be made beautiful other estimable qualities will not secure the wide popularity they deserve. Durable and beautiful colour will always make them salable, and good colour is easily attainable if the value of it is understood.

There are two ways of compassing this necessity. One is to buy, if possible, in piece ends and mill waste, such materials as Turkey red, blue and green ginghams, and blue domestics and denims, as well as all the dark colours which come in tailors' cuttings. The other and better alternative is to buy the waste of white cotton mills and dye it. For the best class of rugs—those which include beauty as well as usefulness, and which will consequently bring a much larger price if sold—it is quite worth while to buy cheap muslins and calicoes; and as quality—that is, coarseness or fineness—is perfectly immaterial, it is possible to buy them at from four to five cents per yard. These goods can be torn lengthwise, which saves nearly the whole labor of sewing them, and from eight to ten yards, according to their fineness, will make a yard of weaving. The best textile for this is undoubtedly unbleached muslin, even approaching the quality called "cheesecloth." This can easily be dyed if one wishes dark instead of light colours, and it makes a light, strong, elastic rug which is very satisfactory.

In rag carpet weaving in homesteads and farmhouses—and it is so truly a domestic art that it is to be hoped this kind of weaving will be confined principally to them—some one of the household should be skilled in simple dyeing. This is very important, as better and cheaper rugs can be made if the weaver can get what she wants in colour by having it dyed in the house, rather than by the chance of finding it among the rags she buys.

CHAPTER III.

DYEING.

In the early years of the past century a dye-tub was as much a necessity in every house as a spinning wheel, and the re-establishment of it in houses where weaving is practised is almost a necessity; in fact, it would be of far greater use at present than in the days when it was only used to dye the wool needed for the family knitting and weaving. All shades of blue, from sky-blue to blue-black, can be dyed in the indigo-tub; and it has the merit of being a cheap as well as an almost perfectly fast dye. It could be used for dyeing warps as well as fillings, and I have before spoken of the difficulty, indeed almost impossibility, of procuring indigo-dyed carpet yarn.

Blue is perhaps more universally useful than any other colour in rag rug making, since it is safe for both cotton and wool, and covers a range from the white rug with blue warp, the blue rug with white warp, through all varieties of shade to the dark blue, or clouded blue, or green rug, upon white warp. It can also be used in connection with yellow or orange, or with copperas or walnut dye, in different shades of green; and, in short, unless one has exceptional advantages in buying rags from woolen mills, I can hardly imagine a profitable industry of rag-weaving established in any farmhouse without the existence of an indigo dyeing-tub.

RED.

The next important color is red. Red warps can be bought, but the lighter shades are not even reasonably fast; and indeed, the only sure way of securing absolutely fast colour in cotton warp is to dye it. Prepared dyes are somewhat expensive on account of the quantity required, but there are two colours, Turkey red and cardinal red, which are extremely good for the purpose. These can be brought at wholesale from dealers in chemicals and dye-stuffs at much cheaper rates than by the small paper from the druggist.

COPPERAS.

The ordinary copperas, which can be bought at any country store, gives a fast nankeen-coloured dye, and this is very useful in making a dull green by an after-dip in the indigo-tub.

WALNUT.

There are some valuable domestic dyes which are within the reach of every country dweller, the best and cheapest of which is walnut or butternut stain. This is made by steeping the bark of the tree or the shell of the nut until the water is dark with colour. It will give various shades of yellow, brown, dark brown and green brown, according to the strength of the decoction or the state of the bark or nut when used. If the bark of the nut is used when green, the result will be a yellow brown; and this stain is also valuable in making a green tint when an after-dip of blue is added. Leaves and tree-bark will give a brown with a very green tint, and these different shades used in different rags woven together give a very agreeably clouded effect. Walnut stain will itself set or fasten some others; for instance, pokeberry stain, which is a lovely crimson, can be made reasonably fast by setting it with walnut juice.

RUST-COLOUR.

Iron rust is the most indelible of all stains besides being a most agreeable yellow, and it is not hard to obtain, as bits of old iron left standing in water will soon manufacture it. It would be a good use for old tin saucepans and various other house utensils which have come to a state of mischievousness instead of usefulness.

GRAY.

Ink gives various shades of gray according to its strength, but it would be cheaper to purchase it in the form of logwood than as ink.

LOGWOOD CHIPS.

Logwood chips boiled in water give a good yellow brown—deep in proportion to the strength of the decoction.

YELLOW FROM FUSTIC.

Yellow from fustic requires to be set with alum, and this is more effectively done if the material to be dyed is soaked in alum water and dried previous to dyeing. Seven ounces of alum to two quarts of water is the proper proportion. The fustic chips should be well soaked, and afterward boiled for a half-hour to extract the dye, which will be a strong and fast yellow.

ORANGE.

Orange is generally the product of annato, which must be dissolved with water to which a lump of washing soda has been added. The material must be soaked in a solution of tin crystals before dipping, if a pure orange is desired, as without this the color will be a pink buff—or "nankeen" color.

What I have written on the subject of home dyeing is intended more in the way of suggestion than direction, as it is simply giving some results of my own experiments, based upon early familiarity with natural growths rather than scientific knowledge. I have found the experiments most interesting, and more than fairly successful, and I can imagine nothing more fascinating than a persistent search for natural and permanent dyes.

The Irish homespun friezes, which are so dependable in colour for out-of-door wear, are invariably dyed with natural stains, procured from heather roots, mosses, and bog plants of like nature. It must be remembered that any permanent or indelible stain is a dye, and if boys and girls who live in the country were set to look for plants possessing the colour-quality, many new ones might be discovered. I am told by a Kentucky mountain woman, used to the production of reliable colour in her excellent weaving, that the ordinary roadside smartweed gives one of the best of yellows. Indeed, she showed me a blanket with a yellow border which had been in use for twenty years, and still held a beautiful lemon yellow. In preparing this, the plant is steeped in water, and the tint set with alum. Combining this with indigo, or by an after-dip in indigo-water, one could procure various shades of fast blue-green, a colour which is hard to get, because most yellows, which should be one of its preparatory tints, are buff instead of lemon yellow.

An unlimited supply and large variety of cheap and reliable colour in rag filling, and a few strong and brilliant colours in warps, are conditions for success in rag rug weaving, but these colours must be studiously and carefully combined to produce the best results.

I have said that, as a rule, light warps must go with dark filling and dark warps with light, and I will add a few general rules which I have found advantageous in my weaving.

In the first place, in rugs which are largely of one colour, as blue, or green, or red, or yellow, no effort should be made to secure *even* dyeing; in fact, the more uneven the colour is the better will be the rug. Dark and light and spotted colour work into a shaded effect which is very attractive. The most successful of the simple rugs I possess is of a cardinal red woven upon a white warp. It was chiefly made of white rags treated with cardinal red Diamond dye, and was purposely made as uneven as possible. The border consists of two four-inch strips of "hit or miss" green, white and red mixed rags, placed four inches from either end, with an inch stripe of red between, and the whole finished with a white knotted fringe.

A safe and general rule is that the border stripes should be of the same colour as the warp—as, for instance, with a red warp a red striped border—while the centre and ends of the rug might be mixed rags of all descriptions.

It is also safe to say that in using pure white or pure black in mixed rags, these two colours, and particularly the white, should appear in short pieces, as otherwise they give a striped instead of a mottled effect, and this is objectionable. White is valuable for strong effects or lines in design; indeed, it is hard to make design prominent or effective except in white or red.

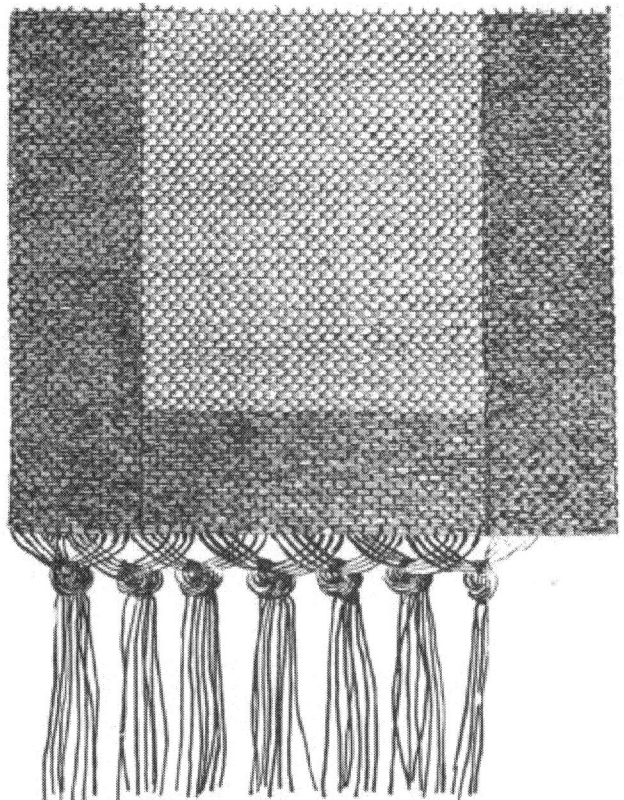

THE LOIS RUG

These few general rules as to colour, together with the particular ones given in other chapters, produce agreeable combinations in very simple and easy fashion. I have not, perhaps, laid as much stress upon warp grouping and treatment as is desirable, since quite distinct effects are produced by these things. Throwing the warp into groups of three or four threads, leaving small spaces between, produces a sort of basket-work style; while simply doubling the warp and holding it with firm tension gives the honeycomb effect of which I have previously spoken. If the filling is wide and soft, and well pushed back between each throw of the shuttle, it will bunch up between the warp threads like a string of beads, and in a dark warp and light filling a rim of coloured shadow seems to show around each little prominence. Such rugs are more elastic to the tread than an even-threaded one, and on the whole may be considered a very desirable variation.

It is well for the weaver to remember that every successful experiment puts the manufacture on a higher plane of development and makes it more valuable as a family industry.

CHAPTER IV.

INGRAIN CARPET RUGS.

Undoubtedly the most useful—and from a utilitarian point of view the most perfect—rag rug is made from worn ingrain carpet, especially if it is of the honest all-wool kind, and not the modern mixture of cotton and wool. There are places in the textile world where a mixture of cotton and wool is highly advantageous, but in ingrain carpeting, where the sympathetic fibre of the wool holds fast to its adopted colour, and the less tenacious cotton allows it to drift easily away, the result is a rusty grayness of colour which shames the whole fabric. This grayness of aspect cannot be overcome in the carpet except by re-dyeing, and even then the improvement may be transitory, so an experienced maker of rugs lets the half-cotton ingrain drift to its end without hope of resurrection.

The cutting of old ingrain into strips for weaving is not so serious a task as it would seem. Where there is an out-of-doors to work in, the breadths can easily be torn apart without inconvenience from dust. After this they should be placed, one at a time, in an old-fashioned "pounding-barrel" and invited to part with every particle of dust which they have accumulated from the foot of man.

For those who do not know the virtues and functions of the "pounding-barrel," I must explain that it is an ordinary, tight, hardwood barrel; the virtue lying in the pounder, which may be a broom-handle, or, what is still better, the smooth old oak or ash handle of a discarded rake or hoe. At the end of it is a firmly fixed block of wood, which can be brought down with vigour upon rough and soiled textiles. It is an effective separator of dust and fibre, and is, in fact, a New England improvement upon the stone-pounding process which one sees along the shores of streams and lakes in nearly all countries but England and America.

If the pounding-barrel is lacking, the next best thing is—after a vigorous shaking—to leave the breadths spread upon the grass, subject to the visitations of wind and rain. After a few days of such exposure they will be quite ready to handle without offense. Then comes the process of cutting. The selvages must be sheared as narrowly as possible, since every inch of the carpet is valuable. When the selvages are removed, the breadths are to be cut into long strips of nearly an inch in width and rolled into balls for the loom. If the pieces are four or five yards in length, only two or three need to be sewn together until the weaving is actually begun, as the balls would otherwise become too heavy to handle. As the work proceeds, however, the joinings must be well lapped and strongly sewn, the rising of one of the ends in the woven piece being a very apparent blemish.

Rugs made of carpeting require a much stronger warp than do ordinary cotton or woolen rugs, and therefore a twine made of flax or hemp, if it be of fast colour, will be found very serviceable. Some weavers fringe the rags by pulling out side threads, and this gives an effect of *nap* to the woven rug which is very effective, for as the rag is doubled in weaving the raveled ends of threads stand up on the surface, making quite a furry appearance. I have a rug treated in this way made from old green carpeting, woven with a red warp, which presents so rich an appearance that it might easily be mistaken for a far more costly one. It has, however, the weak point of having been woven with the ordinary light-red warp of commerce, and is therefore sure to lose colour. If the warp had been re-dyed by the weaver, with "Turkey red," it would probably have held colour as long as it held together.

This cutting of ingrain rags would seem to be a serious task, but where weaving is a business instead of an amusement it is quite worth while to buy a "cutting table" upon which the carpet is stretched and cut with a knife. This table, with its machinery, can be bought wherever looms and loom supplies are kept, at a cost of from seven to eight dollars. If the strips are raveled at all, it should be at least for a third of an inch, as otherwise the rug would possess simply a rough and not a napped surface. If the strips are cut an inch in width and raveled rather more than a third on each side, it still leaves enough cloth to hold firmly in the weaving, but I have known one industrious soul who raveled the strips until only a narrow third was left down the middle of the strip, and this she found it necessary to stitch with the sewing machine to prevent further raveling. I have also known of the experiment of cutting the strips on the bias, stitching along the centre and pulling the two edges until they were completely ruffled. Although this is a painstaking process, it has very tangible merits, as, in the first place, absolutely nothing of the carpet is wasted—no threads are pulled out and thrown away as in the other method—and in the next the sewings together are overhand instead of lapped. The raveled waste can often be used as filling for the ends of rugs if it is wound as it is pulled from the carpet rags. Indeed, one can hardly afford to waste such good material.

It will be seen that there are great possibilities in the carpet rug. Even the unravelled ones are desirable floor covering on account of their weight and firmness. They lie where they are placed, with no turned-up ends, and this is a great virtue in rugs.

Of course much of the beauty of the ingrain carpet rug depends upon the original colour of the carpet. Most of those which are without design will work well into rugs if a strongly contrasting colour is used in the warp. If, for instance, the carpet colour is plain blue, the warp should be white; if yellow, either an orange warp, which will make a very bright rug, or a green warp, which will give a soft yellowish green, or a blue, which will give a general effect of green changing to yellow.

If the carpet should be a figured one, a red warp will be found more effective than any other in bringing all the colours together. If it should happen to be faded or colourless, the breadths can be dipped in a tub of strong dye of some colour which will act well upon the previous tint. If, for instance, it should be a faded blue, it may be dipped in an indigo dye for renewal of colour, or into yellow, which will change it into green. A poor yellow will take a brilliant red dye, and a faded brown or fawn will be changed into a good claret colour by treating it with red dye. Faded brown or fawn colours will take a good dark green, as will also a weak blue. Blue can also be treated with yellow or a fresher blue.

Of course, in speaking of this kind of dyeing, the renewal of old tints, it is with reference to the common prepared dyes which are for sale—with directions—by every druggist, and with a little knowledge of how these colours act upon each other one can produce very good effects. It is quite a different thing from the dyeing of fibre which is to be woven into cloth. In the latter case it is far wiser to use vegetable dyes, but in the freshening of old material the prepared mineral dyes are more convenient and sufficiently effective.

CHAPTER V.

WOVEN RAG PORTIERES.

Rag weaving is not necessarily confined to rugs, for very beautiful portieres and table and lounge covers may be woven from carefully chosen and prepared rags. The process is practically the same, the difference being like that between coarse and fine needlework, where finer material and closer and more painstaking handiwork is bestowed. The result is like a homespun cloth. Both warp and woof must be finer than in ordinary carpet weaving. Instead of coarse cotton yarn, warp must be fine "mercerized" cotton, or of linen or silk thread, and the warp threads are set much closer in the loom. In place of ten or twelve threads to the inch, there should be from fifteen to twenty. The woof or filling may be old or new, and either of fine cotton, merino, serge, or other wool material, or of silk. The ordinary "silk-rag portiere" is not a very attractive hanging, being somewhat akin to the crazy quilt, and made, as is that bewildering production, from a collection of ribbons and silk pieces of all colours and qualities, cut and sewed together in a haphazard way, without any arrangement of colour or thought of effect, and sent to the weaver with a vague idea of getting something of worth from valueless material. This is quite a different thing from a silk portiere made from some beautiful old silk garment, which is too much worn for further use, where warp and woof colour are selected for fitness and harmony, and the weaver uses her rags, as the painter does his colours, with a purpose of artistic effect. If the work is done from that point of view, the last state of the once beautiful old garment may truly be said to be better than the first. If a light cloth is used for this kind of manufacture, it may be torn into strips so narrow as to simulate yarn—and make what appears to be yarn weaving. This cannot well be done with old or worn cloth, because there is not strength in the very narrow strip to bear the strain of tearing; but new muslin, almost as light as that which is known as "cheesecloth," treated in this way makes a beautiful canvas-like weaving which, if well coloured, is very attractive for portieres or table covers.

If one has breadths of silk of a quality which can be torn without raveling, and is sufficiently strong to bear the process, it is delightful material to work with. If it is of ordinary thickness, a half-inch in width is quite wide enough, and this will roll or double into the size of ordinary yarn. If the silk is not strong enough to tear, it is better to cut the strips upon the bias than straight, and the same is true of fine woolens, like merinos, cashmeres, or any worsted goods. There is much more elasticity in them when cut in this way, and they are more readily crushed together by the warp.

I know a beautiful hanging of crimson silk, or rather of crimson and garnet—the crimson having been originally a light silk dress dyed to shade into the garnet. The two coloured rags were sewn together "hit or miss" fashion and woven upon a bright cardinal-coloured warp. There was no attempt at border: it was simply a length of vari-coloured coarse silk weaving, absolutely precious for colour and quality.

Treated in this way, an old silk gown takes on quite a new value and becomes invested with absorbing interest. Spots and tarnish disappear in the metempsychosis, or serve for scattered variation, and if the weaver chooses to still further embellish it with a monogram or design in cross stitch embroidery, she has acquired a piece of drapery which might be a valuable inheritance to her children.

Merino or cashmere which has been worn and washed, and is coupled with other material of harmonizing colour, like pieces of silk or velvet, is almost as valuable for the making of portieres and table covers as if it were silk. Indeed, for the latter purpose it is preferable, being generally washable.

Cotton hangings made in this way are often very desirable. "Summer muslins" which have served their time as dresses, and are of beautiful colour and quite strong enough to go into the loom, can be woven with a warp of gray linen thread into really beautiful hangings, especially the strong, plain tints—the blues and greens and reds which have been so much worn of late years. They have the advantage of being easily washable, and are particularly suitable for country-house hangings. Even worn sheets and pillow-cases can be dyed to suit the furnishing of different rooms, and woven with a silk warp of stronger colour. They should be torn into strips not more than a third of an inch wide, so that it may crush into a roll not larger than an ordinary yarn. This will weave into a light, strong cloth, always interesting because it differs from anything which can be purchased through ordinary channels. To reappear in the shape of a beautiful and valuable rag-weaving is the final resurrection of good textiles, when they have performed their duty in the world and been worn out in its service.

These home-woven portieres are better without borders, the whole surface being plain or simply clouded by mixing two tints of the same colour together. They can be elaborated by adding a hand-made fringe of folds of cloth sewn into a lattice and finished with tassels. This is quite a decorative feature, and particularly suitable to the weaving.

It can easily be understood that a large share of the beauty of making these household furnishings lies in the colour. If that is good the rug or portiere or table-cover is beautiful. If it is either dull or glaring, the pleasure one might have in it is lacking, and it is quite within one's power to have the article always beautiful.

It must also be remembered, if weaving is taken up as a source of profit, that *few things which do not please the eye will sell.* Therefore, if for no other reason, it is well worth while for the weaver to first study the choice, production and combination of beautiful colours rather than the fabric of the rug.

I have said, and will reiterate, that for this particular kind of manufacture—the restoration and adaptation of old goods, and the strengthening of tints in carpet warps—the yellows and reds of the Magic or Diamond dyes of commerce are effective and reliable. Indeed, for new goods cardinal dye is all that could be asked, but when it comes to the use of dyes for the weaving of textiles and artistic fabrics, one must resort to dye woods and plants.

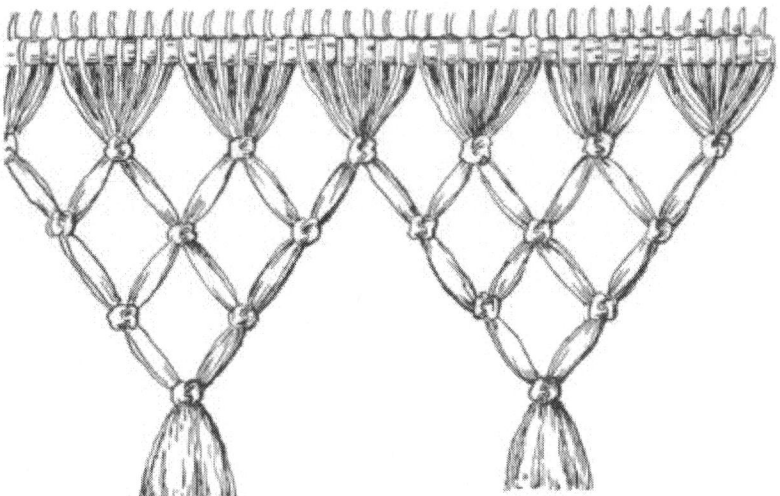

KNOTTED WARP FRINGE FOR WOVEN TABLE-COVER

How To Make Rugs

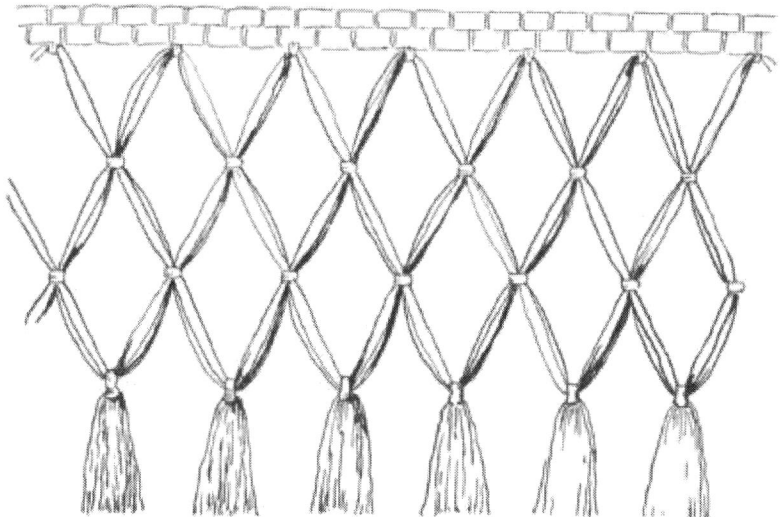

SEWED RAG FRINGE FOR WOVEN PORTIERE

FRINGES.

Nothing is more important than the proper *finish* of the rug, and this generally consists in a careful going over of the work after it has come from the loom—the cutting of stray ravelings and sewing of loose ends, and the knotting of the long warp ends.

It is only a very careless or inexperienced weaver who leaves the warp ends in the state in which they come from the loom; and indeed they can be made one of the most effective features of the rug. Simple knotting of every six threads will make them safe from raveling, and sometimes the shortness of the warp ends allows no more than this. It is well worth while, however, to leave six or eight inches to work into decorative fringes, and these can be made in various ways, of which illustrations are given.

In the case of decorative fringes there can be double or triple knotting—straight, or worked into points; braided fringes which have the merit of both strength and beauty, and are free from the tangle-trouble of long fringes, and the very effective rag-lattice finish for portieres and table-covers. Indeed, half the beauty of the rug may lie in the fringing and finish.

PROFITS.

The pecuniary gain from rag rug weaving may easily be calculated. First of all comes the cost of the loom, which will be about seventy dollars. The interest upon this, with necessary repairs, may be reckoned at about five dollars per year.

To every six-foot rug goes two-thirds of a pound of warp, and this would amount to from ten-and-a-half to fourteen cents, according to the rate of purchase. To every such rug must go three pounds of cotton or two pounds of woolen rags, costing for cotton thirty and for woolen fifty cents. To the cotton rugs must be added the possible cost of dye-stuffs, which, again, might cost twenty cents, making cost of material in either cotton or woolen rugs from sixty to sixty-four cents.

As far as profit is concerned, if rag rugs are well made they will sell for two dollars each, if successful in colour, from two dollars and a half to three and a half, and if beautiful and exceptional in colour and finish from four to six dollars. But it must be remembered that this latter price will be for rugs which have artistic value. Probably the average weaver can safely reckon upon one dollar and eighty-five cents to two dollars regular profit for the labor of sewing and filling and weaving and knotting the rugs. It is fair to accept this as a basis for regular profit, the amount of which must depend upon facility of production and the ability to produce unexceptionable things.

But it is not alone pecuniary gain which should be considered. Ability to produce or create a good thing is in itself a happiness, and the value of happiness cannot easily be reckoned. The knowledge necessary to such production is a personal gain. Everything we can do which people generally cannot or do not do, or which we can do better than others, helps us to a certain value of ourselves which makes life valuable. For this reason, then, as well as for the gain of it, a loom in the house and a knowledge of weaving is an advantage, not only for the elders, but to the children. If the boys and girls in every farmhouse were taught to create more things, they would not only be abler as human beings, but they would not be so ready to run out into the world in search of interesting occupations. A loom, a turning-lathe, a work-bench, and a chest of tools, a house-organ or melodeon, and a neighbourhood library, would keep boys and girls at home, and make them more valuable citizens when independent living became a necessity. Everything which broadens the life, which must by reason of narrow means and fixed occupation be stationary, gives something of the advantage of travel and contact with the world, and the adding of profitable outside industries to farmhouse life is an important step in this direction.

CHAPTER VI.

WOOLEN RUGS.

There are two conditions which will make home weaving valuable. The first is that the material, whether it be of cotton or wool, should be grown upon the farm, and that it could not be sold in the raw state at a price which would make the growing of it profitable. In wool crops there are certain odds and ends of ragged, stained and torn locks, which would injure the appearance of the fleece, and are therefore thrown aside, and this waste is perfectly suitable for rug weaving.

In cotton there is not the amount of waste, but the fibre itself is not as valuable, and a portion of it could be reserved for home weaving, even though it should not be turned to more profitable account.

The next condition is that the time used in weaving is also waste or left-over time. If housekeeping requires only a quarter or half of a woman's time, weaving is more restful and interesting, as well as more profitable, than idleness; and in almost every family there are members to whom partial employment would be a boon.

There is no marketable value for spare time or for individual taste, so that the women of the family possessing these can start a weaving enterprise, counting only the cost of material at growers' prices. If they can card, spin, dye and weave as well as the women of two generations did before them, they have a most profitable industry in their own hands in the shape of weaving.

If materials must be purchased the profit is smaller, and the question arises whether spare time and personal taste and skill can be made profitable. This depends entirely upon circumstances and character. When circumstances are or can be made favourable, and there is industry and ambition behind them, domestic weaving is a beautiful and profitable occupation.

There are many neighbourhoods where the conditions are exactly suitable to the prosecution of important domestic industries—localities where sheep are raised and wool is a regular product, or where cotton is grown and the weaving habit is not extinct. This is true of many New England neighbourhoods and of the whole Cumberland Mountain region, and it is in response to a demand for direction of unapplied advantages that this book is written.

I am convinced that the weaving of domestic wool or cotton rugs might be so developed in the mountain regions of the South as to greatly decrease the importation of Eastern ones of the same grade.

An endless variety might be made in these localities, the difference of climate, material and habits of thought adding interest as well as variety, and it is safe to say that the home market is waiting for them. Housekeepers have learned by experience that a rug which can be easily lifted and frequently shaken is not only far more cleanly, and consequently safer, from a sanitary point of view, than a carpet, but that it has other merits which are of economic as well as esthetic importance.

A rug is more durable than a carpet of equal weight and texture because it can be constantly shifted from points of wear to those which are less exposed. It can be moved from room to room, or even from house to house, without the trouble of shaping or fitting; and last but not least, it brings a concentration of colour exactly where it is needed for effect, and this is possible to no other piece of house furnishing. In short, there seems to be no bar to its general acceptance, excepting the bad floors of our immediate predecessors in building.

It only needs that cost, quality and general effect of the home-woven rugs should be shaped into perfect adaptation to our wants, to make them as necessary a part of ordinary house-furnishing as chairs and tables.

These three requirements are within the reach of any home-weaving farmer's wife who will give to the work the same thought for economical conditions, the same ambition for thorough work and the same intelligent study which her husband bestows upon his successful farming.

As there is already one American rug which fulfills most of these conditions, it is well to consider it as a starting point for progress. This is the heavy Indian rug known as the Navajo blanket. Originally fashioned to withstand the cold and exposure of outdoor life, it has combined thickness, durability and softness with excellent colour and weaving and perfectly characteristic design.

In the best examples, where the wool is not bought from traders, but carded, spun and dyed by the weaver, the Navajo blanket is a perfect production of its kind, and I cannot help wondering that the manufacture of these rug-like blankets—some of which are of great intrinsic value—should have been so long confined to a primitive race, living at our very doors. The whole process of spinning, dyeing and weaving could be carried on in any farmhouse, using the coarsest and least valuable wool, and by reliable and well-chosen colour, good weight and careful weaving bringing the manufacture into a prominent place among the home productions of our people.

One can hardly imagine simpler machinery than is used by the Indians. It is scarcely more than a parallelogram of sticks, supported by a back brace, and yet upon these simple looms an Indian woman will weave a fabric that will actually hold water.

The clumsy, old-fashioned loom which is still in use in many farmhouses is fully equal to all demands of this variety of weaving, but there are already in the market steel-frame looms with fly shuttles which take up much less room and are more easily worked. I was about to say they were capable of better work, but nothing could be better in method than the Indian rug, woven on its three upright sticks; and after all it is well to remember that *quality is in the weaver*, and not in the loom. The results obtained from the simplest machinery can be made to cover ground which is truly artistic.

As an example of what may be done to make this kind of weaving available, we will suppose that some one having an ordinary loom, and in the habit of weaving rag carpet, wishes to experiment toward the production of a good yarn rug. The first thing required would, of course, be material for both warp and woof.

The warp can be made of strong cotton yarn which is manufactured for this very purpose and can be bought for about seventeen cents a pound. This is probably cheaper than it could be carded and spun at home even on a cotton-growing farm.

The wool filling should be coarse and slack-twisted, and on wool-growing farms or in wool-growing districts is easily produced. If it is of home manufacture, it may be spun as loosely or slackly as possible, dyed and woven without doubling, which will be seen to be an economy of labor. The single thread, slackly twisted, gives a very desirable elasticity to the fabric, because the wool fibre is not too closely bound or packed. On the other hand, if the wool as well as the warp must be bought, it is best to get it from the spinning machine in its first state of the single thread, and do the doubling and twisting at home. In this case it can be doubled as many or as few times as it is thought best, and twisted as little as possible.

The next and most important thing is colour, and it is a great advantage if the dyeing can be done at home. There is a strong and well-founded preference among art producers in favor of vegetable dyes, and yet it is possible to use certain of the aniline colours, especially in combination, in safe and satisfactory ways.

Every one who undertakes domestic weaving must know how to dye one or two good colours—black, of course, and the half-black or gray which a good colourist of my acquaintance calls *light black*; indigo blue equally, of course, in three shades of very dark, medium and light; and red in two shades of dark and light. Here are seven shades from the three dyes, and when we add white we see that the weaver is already very well equipped with a variety of colour. The eight shades can be still further enlarged by clouding and mixing. The mixing can be done in two ways, either by carding two tints together before spinning, or by twisting them together when spun.

Carding together gives a very much better effect in wool, while twisting together is preferable in cotton.

Dark blue and white or medium blue and white wool carded together will give two blue-grays, which cannot be obtained by dyeing, and are most valuable. White and red carded together give a lovely pink, and any shade of gray can be made by carding different proportions of black and white or half-black and white. A valuable gray is made by carding black and white wool together (and by black wool I mean the natural black or brownish wool of black sheep). Mixing of deeply dyed and white wool together in carding is, artistically considered, a very valuable process, as it gives a softness of colour which it is impossible to get in any other way. Clouding—which is almost an indispensable process for rug centres—can be done by winding certain portions of the skeins or hanks of yarn very tightly and closely with twine before they are thrown into the dye-pot. The winding must be close enough to prevent the dye penetrating to the yarn. This means, of course, when the clouding is to be of white and another colour. If it is to be of two shades of one colour, as a light and medium blue, the skein is first dyed a light blue, and after drying is wound as I have described, and thrown again into the dye-pot, until the unwound portions become the darker blue which we call medium.

In a neighbourhood where weaving is a general industry, it is an advantage if some one person who has a general aptitude for dyeing and experiments in colours undertakes it as a business. This is on the principle that a person who does only one thing does it with more facility and better than one who works in various lines. Yet even when there is a neighbourhood dyer, it is, as I have said, almost indispensable that the weaver should know how to dye one or two colours and to do it well.

Supposing that the material, in the shape of coarse cotton warp, black, red or white, has been secured, or that a wool filling in the colours and shades I have described has been prepared for weaving; the loom is then to be warped, at the rate of fifteen or less threads to the inch, according to the coarseness or fineness of the filling.

It is well to weave a half-inch of the cotton warp for filling, as this binds the ends more firmly than wool. Next to this, a border of black and gray in alternate half-inch stripes can be woven, and following that, the body of the rug in dark red, clouded with white. After five feet of the red is woven, a border end of the black and gray is added, and the rug may be cut from the loom, leaving about four inches of the warp at either end as a fringe. If the filling yarn is of good colour, and has been well packed in the weaving, *so as to entirely cover the warp*, the result will be a good, attractive and durable woolen rug, woven after the Navajo method.

In this one example I have given the bare and simple outline by following which a weaver whose previous work has been only rag carpet weaving can manufacture a good and valuable wool rug. The difference will be simply that of close warping and a substitution of wool for rags. Its value will be considerably increased or lessened by the choice of material both in quality and colour and the closeness and perfection of weaving.

The example given calls for a rug six feet long by three feet in width. To make this very rug a much more important one, it needs only to vary the size of the border. For a larger rug the length must be increased two feet, and the border, which in this case must be of plain or mixed black—that is, it must not be alternated with stripes of gray—must measure one foot at either end. When this is complete, two narrow strips one foot in width, woven with mixed black filling, must be sewed on either side, making a rug eight feet long and five in width. It is not a disadvantage to have this border strip sewn, instead of being woven as a part of the centre. Many of the cheaper Oriental weavings are put together in this way, and as many of the older house-looms will only weave a three-foot width, it is well to know that that need not prevent the production of rugs of considerable size.

Endless variations of this very simple yarn rug can be made with variation in size as well as in colour. Two breadths and two borders, the breadths three feet in width and the borders one foot and six inches, will give a breadth of nine feet, which with a corresponding length will give a rug which will sufficiently cover the floor of an ordinary room. If the centre is skilfully mottled and shaded, it will make a floor spread of beautiful colour, and one which could hardly be found in shops.

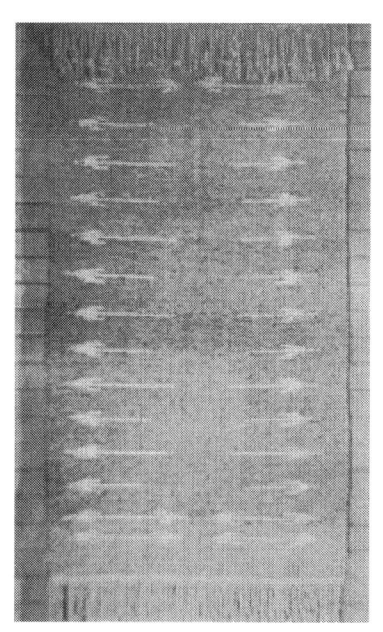

ISLE LA MOTTE RUG

The border can be made brighter, as well as firmer and stiffer, by using two filling threads together—a red and a black; or an alternate use of red and black, using two shuttles, will give a lighter and better effect than when black is used exclusively.

After size and weight—or, to speak comprehensively, *quality*—is secured in this kind of simple weaving, the next most important thing is colour. Of course the colour must be absolutely fast, but I have shown how much variety can be made by shading and mixing of three fast colours, and much more subtle and artistic effects can be produced by weaving alternate threads of different colours. Indeed, the effects obtained by using alternate threads can be varied to almost any extent; as, for instance, a blue and yellow thread—provided the blue is no deeper than the yellow—will give the effect of green to the eye. If the blue is stronger or deeper, as it will almost necessarily be, it will be modified and softened into a greenish blue.

Red and white woven in alternate threads upon a white warp will give an effect of pink, and with this colour for a centre the border should be a good gray.

Of course, alternate throwing of different coloured yarns makes the weaving go more slowly than when one alone is used, and something of the same colour effect can be produced by doubling, instead of alternating. It is, of course, not quite the same, as one colour may show either under or over the other, and the effect is apt to be mottled instead of one of uniform stripes.

The end in view in all these mixtures is *variation* and liveliness of colour, not an effect of stripes or spots; indeed, these are very objectionable, especially when in contrasted or different colors. A deepening or lightening of the same colour in irregular patches, as will occur in clouded yarns, gives interest, whereas if these cloudings were in strongly contrasted colours they would be crude and unrestful. For this reason, if for no other, it is well to work in few tints, and use contrasting colours only for borders.

To show how much variety is possible in weaving with the few dyes I have named, I will give a number of combinations which will produce good results and be apt to harmonize with ordinary furnishing. By adding orange yellow, which is also one of the simplest and safest of dyes, we secure by mixture with blue a mottled green, and this completes a range of colour which really leaves nothing to be desired.

No. 1. *Colours black and red.* Border, alternate stripes of black and dark red, as follows: First stripe of black, one and a half inches; second stripe of red, one inch; third stripe of black, one inch; fourth stripe of red, one-half inch; fifth stripe of black, three-quarters inch; sixth stripe of red, one-half inch; seventh stripe of black, half-inch; centre of light red clouded with dark red; reversed border.

No. 2. *Colours black and red.* Border one foot in depth, of black and red threads woven alternately. Centre dark red, clouded with light red. Woven six feet, with one-foot border at sides as well as ends.

No. 3. *Colours red and white.* Border seven inches of plain red. Centre of red and white woven alternately.

No. 4. *Colours red and black.* Border black and red, threads woven alternately, one foot in depth; centre of alternate stripes, two inches in width, of dark red and light red; eight feet in length, with foot-wide side borders, woven with alternate threads of red and black.

No. 5. *Colours red and black.* Border eighteen inches in depth, of alternate red and black, half-inch stripes. Centre of dark red, clouded with light.

No. 6. *Colours gray, red and white*, to be woven of doubled, slightly twisted threads. Border one foot in depth at ends and sides, woven of red and gray yarn twisted together. Centre of red and white yarn in twisted threads.

No. 7. *Colours red and white.* Border of plain red, twenty inches in depth. Centre in alternate half-inch stripes of red and white.

No. 8. *Colours blue, red and black.* Border four inches deep of black, two inches of plain red, one inch of black. Centre of clouded blue.

No. 9. *Colour blue.* Border eight inches of darkest blue. Centre of clouded medium and light blue.

No. 10. *Colours blue and white.* Border of very dark and medium blue woven together. Centre of blue and white yarn woven together.

No. 11. *Colours blue and white.* Border of medium plain blue. Centre of blue, clouded with white.

No. 12. *Colours blue and white.* Border of medium blue. Centre of alternate stripes of one inch width blue, and half-inch white stripes.

No. 13. *Colours blue and white.* Border twelve inches deep of dark blue, clouded with medium. Centre of alternate threads of medium blue and white.

No. 14. *Colours blue, black and orange yellow.* Border eight inches deep of black, one inch of orange, two of black. Centre, alternate threads of blue and orange.

No. 15. Border of doubled threads of dark blue and orange. Centre of alternate stripes of inch wide light blue and orange woven together, one-half inch stripes of clear orange and white woven together.

In the examples I have given, wherever doubled threads of different colours woven together are used, it must be understood that they are to be slightly twisted, and that the warping for double-filling rugs need not be as close as for single filling. Twelve threads to the inch would be better than fifteen, and perhaps ten or eleven would be still better. Doubled yarn of different colours produces a mottled or broken effect, and this can often be done where the colours of the yarns do not quite satisfy the weaver. If they are too dull, twisting them slackly with a very brilliant tint will give a better shade than if the original tint was satisfactory, but in the same way yarns which are too brilliant can often be made soft and effective by twisting them together with a paler tint. Minute particles of colour brought together in this way are brilliant without crudeness. It is, in fact, the very principle upon which impressionist painters work, giving pure colour instead of mixed, but in such minute and broken bits that the eye confounds them with surrounding colour, getting at the same time the double impression of softness and vivacity.

These examples of fifteen different rugs which can be woven from the three tints of blue, red and orange, together with black and white, do not by any means exhaust the possibilities of variety which can be obtained from three tints. Each rug will give a suggestion for the next, and each may be an improvement upon its predecessor.

CHAPTER VII.

COTTON RUGS.

The warp-covered weaving which I have described in a previous chapter as being the simplest and best method for woolen rugs, is equally applicable to cotton weaving. It is, in fact, the one used in making the cotton rugs woven in prisons in India, and which in consequence are known as "prison rugs." They are generally woven in stripes of dark and light shades of indigo blue and measure about four by eight feet. They are greatly used by English residents in India, being much better adapted to life in a hot climate than the more costly Indian and Persian rugs, which supply the world-demand for floor coverings.

In our own summer climate and chintz-furnished summer cottages they would be an extremely appropriate and economical covering for floors. The warp is like that of the Navajo blanket, a heavy cotton cord, the filling or woof of many doubled fine cotton threads, which quite cover the heavy warp, and give the ridged effect of a coarse *rep*.

As I have said, they are woven almost invariably in horizontal stripes of two blues, or blue and white, with darker ends and a warp fringe. Simple as they are and indeed must be, as they are the result of unskilled labour, they are pleasant to look at, and have many virtues not dependent upon looks. They are warm and pleasant to unshod feet, and therefore suitable for bedroom use. They are soft to shoe tread, and give colour and comfort to a summer piazza. They can be hung as portieres in draughty places with a certainty of shelter, and can be lifted and thrown upon the grass to be washed by the downpour of a thunder shower, and left to dry in the sun without detriment to colour or quality.

Surely this is a goodly list of virtues, and the sum of them is by no means exhausted. Their durability is surprising; and they can be sewn together and stretched upon large floors with excellent colour effect. They can be turned or moved from room to room and place to place with a facility which makes them more than useful. The manufacture is so simple that a child might weave them, while at the same time, by a skilful use of colour and good arrangement of border, they can be made to fit the needs of the most luxurious as well as the simplest summer cottage. In short, they are capable of infinite variation and improvement, without departure from the simple method of the "prison rug."

Of course the variation must be in colour and the arrangement of colour; and in studying this possible improvement it must be remembered that cotton will neither take nor hold dyes as readily as wool or silk, and that certain dyes which are very tenacious in their hold upon animal fibre cannot be depended upon when applied to vegetable fibre. There are, however, certain dyes upon which we can safely rely. Indigo blue, and the red used in dyeing what is called Turkey red, are reliable in application to both wool and cotton, and are water and sun proof as well. Walnut and butternut stains will give fast shades of brown and yellow, and in addition there is also the buff or nankeen-coloured cotton, the natural tint of which combines well with brown and blue.

In giving directions for rug colourings in cottons, I shall confine myself to the use of black, white, blue and red, because these colours are easily procurable, and also because rugs manufactured from them will fit the style of furnishing which demands cotton rugs.

The examples I shall give call for graduated dyeing, especially in the two tints of red and blue.

Any one expecting to succeed in rug weaving must be able to procure or produce from two to three planes of colour, as well as two mixtures in each. These would be as follows:

In blue:—1st, dark blue; 2d, medium blue; 3d, light blue.

After these three tints are secure, three variations of blue can be made by knotting the skeins more or less closely and throwing medium, light blue and white together into the dye-tub. Here they must remain until the white skeins show an outside of light blue; the light blue skeins are apparently changed to medium, and the medium to dark. When they are untied and dried they will show three clouded mixtures:

1st, the medium blue clouded with dark; 2d, light blue clouded with medium blue; 3d, white, clouded with light blue.

Here we have six variations of the one tint. Red can be treated in the same way, except that a rather light and a very dark red are all that can be counted upon safely as plain tints. A very light red will not hold. Therefore we have in reds:—1st, dark red; 2d, light red; 3d, light red, clouded with dark; 4th, white, clouded with light red.

This gives ten shades in these two tints, and when we add the variations which seem to come of themselves in dyeing, variations which are by no means subject to rule, we shall see that with these two, and black and white, we are very well equipped.

The more irregular the clouding, the better the results. The yarn may be made into large double knots, or small single ones, or into more or less tightly wound balls or bundles, and each will have its own special and peculiar effect. Perhaps it is well to say that in clouding upon white the colours should be kept as light as is consistent with the tenacity of tint.

After clouding, still another process in cotton mixtures is possible, and this is in "doubling and twisting," which has the effect of darkening or lightening any tint at will, as well as of giving a mottled instead of a plain surface.

Having secured variety by these various expedients, the next step is to make harmonious and well-balanced combinations, and this is quite as important, or even more so, as mere variety.

There is one very simple and useful rule in colour arrangements, and this is to make one tint largely predominant. If it is to be a blue rug, or a pink, or a white one, use other colours only to *emphasize* the predominant one, as, for instance, a blue rug may be emphasized by a border of red and black; or a red rug by a border of black and white, or black and yellow.

The border should always be stronger—that is darker or deeper in colour—than the centre, even when the same colour is used throughout, as in a light red rug, with dark, almost claret-red ends, or a medium blue rug with very dark blue ends.

White, however, can often be used in borders of rather dark rugs in alternation with black or any dark colour, because its total absence of tint makes it strong and distinct, and gives it *force* in marking a limit.

One successful combination of colours will suggest others, and the weaver who has taken pains to provide herself with a variety of shades, and will follow the rules of proportion, will be at no loss in laying out the plan of her weavings.

The examples for fifteen weavings given in the paper on wool rugs are equally available in cotton. I will, however, add a few variations especially adapted for cotton rugs:

No. 1. *Colours blue and white.* Border six inches of plain dark blue. Six inches of alternate half-inch stripes of dark blue and white. Four to five feet of clouded blue, border repeated, with four inches of warp fringe as a finish.

No. 2. *Colours blue and white.* Border eight inches wide of plain medium blue. Centre, six feet of light blue, clouded with medium. Two side borders eight inches wide; finish of white warp fringe.

No. 3. *Colours black, white and red.* Border twelve inches of alternate half-inch stripes of black and white. Centre, four feet of light red, clouded with dark. Repeat border, and finish with warp fringe.

No. 4. *Colours red and white.* Border, twelve inches of dark and light red, in twisted double thread. Centre, light red and white twisted double thread. Repeat border and finish with four-inch fringe.

No. 5. *Colours butternut-brown, walnut-yellow, red, and white.* Border of six inches of brown and yellow, twisted together. Centre, five feet of light red and white, twisted together. Repeat border, and finish with fringe.

No. 6. *Colours brown, blue, and clouded-white.* Border, half-inch stripes of medium blue and brown alternated for six inches. Centre, five feet of light blue, clouded with medium. Repeat border and finish with warp fringe.

These six examples may be varied to any extent by the use of clouded, plain or mixed centres. Borders, as a rule, should be woven of unclouded colours.

A natural development of the cotton rug would be the weaving of coarse cotton yarns into piece lengths which could be cut and sewn like ingrain carpet, or like the fine cotton-warped mattings which have been so popular of late years. They would have the advantage over grass-weavings in durability, ease of handling and liveliness of effect. Indeed, the latter consideration is of great importance, as cotton carpets can be woven to harmonize with the chintzes and cottons which are so much used in summer furnishings. This is especially true of indigo-blue floor covering, since so few things are absolutely perfect as an adjunct to the blue chambrays, striped awning-cloths, denims, and India prints so constantly and effectively used in draperies. Indeed, such excellent art in design has been devoted to blue prints, both foreign and domestic, that one can safely reckon upon their prolonged use, and this being taken for granted, it is well to extend the weaving of mixtures of white and blue indefinitely.

Although the warp-covered method described for woolen and cotton rug weaving can very well be used for carpets, the still simpler one of the alternate thread, or basket-weaving, when warp and filling are of equal weight and size, can be made to answer the purpose quite as well. In fact, there is a certain advantage in the latter method, since it makes the warp a factor in the arrangement of colour.

It is necessary in this style of weaving that the filling should be a hand-twisted thread of the same weight and size as the warp, and of a lighter or darker shade of the same colour. If the warp is dark, the filling may be light, or the reverse. It should be warped at the rate of about twenty-four threads to the inch.

In this kind of weaving the colours must be plain—that is, unclouded—as the variation is obtained by the different shades of warp and filling. Still another variation is made by using a closer warp of thirty threads to the inch and a large soft vari-colour filling which will show between the warp threads with a peculiar watered or vibratory effect. A light red warp, with a very loosely twisted filling of black and white, or a medium blue warp with a black and orange filling, will give extremely good results.

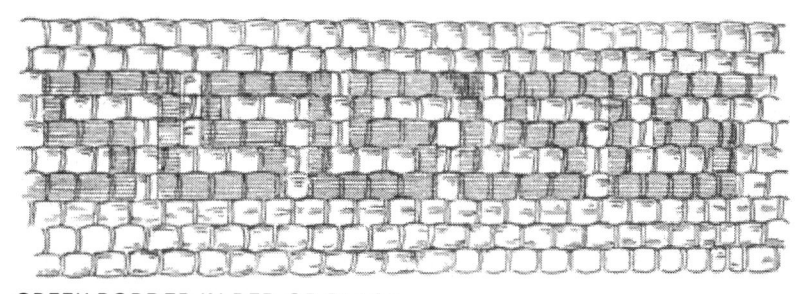

GREEK BORDER IN RED OR BLACK

BRAIDED FRINGE

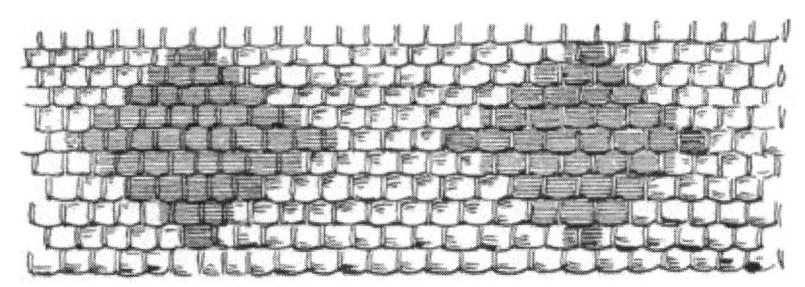

DIAMOND BORDER IN RED OR BLACK

What I have said thus far as to the weaving of woolen and cotton rugs, and of cotton carpets, gives practical directions for artistic results to women who understand the use of the loom in very simple weaving. Of course, more difficult things can be done even with ordinary looms, as any one who has examined the elaborate blue-and-white spreads our grandmothers wove upon the cumbrous house-loom of that period can testify. In fact, the degree of skill required in the weaving of these precious heirlooms would be quite sufficient for the production of rugs adapted to very exacting purchasers.

Perhaps it is as well to add that the directions given in this and the preceding chapter for rug weaving are designed not only or exclusively for weavers, but also for club women who are so situated as to have access to and influence in farming or weaving neighbourhoods.

Home manufactures, guided by women of culture and means, would have the advantage not only of refinement of taste, but of a certainty of aim. Women know what women like, and as they are the final purchasers of all household furnishings, they are not apt to encourage the making of things for which there is no demand.

I am often asked the question, How are all of these homespun and home-woven things to be disposed of? To this I answer that the first effort of the promoters or originators must be—*to fit them for an existing demand*.

There is no doubt of the genuineness of a demand for special domestic weavings. Any neighbourhood or combination of women known to be able to furnish such articles to the public would find the want far in excess of the supply, simply because undirected or commercial manufactures cannot fit personal wants as perfectly as special things can do. It must be remembered, also, that the interchange of news between bodies of women interested in industrial art will be a very potent factor in the creation of a market for any domestic specialty. In fact, it is in response to a demand that these articles upon home-weavings have been prepared, and a demand for technical instruction presupposes an interest in the result.

CHAPTER VIII.

LINSEY WOOLSEY.

It has often been given as a reason for the discontinuance of home weaving, that no product of the hand loom can be as exact or as cheap as that of the power loom. The statement as to cost and quality is true, but so far from being a discouraging one, it gives actual reasons for the continuance of domestic weavings. The very fact that homespun textiles are not exact—in the sense of absolute sameness—and not cheap, in the sense of first cost, is apt to be a reason for buying them. Hand-weaving, like handwriting, is individual, and this is a virtue instead of a defect, since it gives the variety which satisfies some mystery of human liking, a preference for inequality rather than monotonous excellence.

Every hand-woven web differs from every other one in certain characteristics which are stamped upon it by the weaver, and we value these differences. In fact, this very trace of human individuality is the initial charm belonging to all art industries, and even if we discount this advantage, and reckon only money cost and money value, durability must certainly count for something. A thing which costs more and lasts longer is as cheap as one which costs less and goes to pieces before its proper time.

In a long and intimate acquaintance with what are called "art textiles"—that is, textiles which satisfy the eye and the imagination and fulfill more or less competently the function of use, I have learned that certain very desirable qualities are more often found in home-woven than in machine-woven goods. Something is wanting in each of the excellent and wonderful variety of commercial manufactures which would fit it for the various decorative and art processes which modern life demands. To perfectly satisfy this demand, we should have a weaving which is not only in itself an artistic manufacture, but which easily absorbs any additional application of art.

In my own mind I call the thing which might and does not exist, The Missing Textile. To make it entirely appropriate to our esthetic and practical needs, the missing textile must be strong enough for every-day wear and use; it must be capable of soft, round folds in hanging; and have the quality of elasticity which will prevent creasing; and above all, it must have beautiful and lasting colour. If it can add to these qualities an adaptability to various household uses, it will achieve success and deserve it. These different qualities, and especially the one of a natural affinity for such art-processes as colour and embroidery, exist in none of our domestic weavings, excepting only linsey woolsey. After much study of this virtuous product of the mountain regions of our Southern States I find it capable of great development. It has two qualities which are not often co-existent, and these are strength and flexibility; and this is owing not only to its being hand-woven, but also to its being a wool-filled textile—that is, it is woven upon a cotton warp, with a single twisted wool-filling. This peculiarity of texture makes it very suitable for embroidery, since it offers little resistance to the needle, and yet is firm enough to prevent stitches sinking into its substance—a frequent fault with soft or loosely woven textiles. The warp is generally made of what the weavers call mill yarns, cotton yarns spun and often dyed in cotton mills; and when the cloth is woven for women's wear it is apt to carry a striped warp of red and blue, with a mixed filling made from spinning the wool of black sheep with a small proportion of white.

In searching for art textiles, one would not find much encouragement in this particular variety of linsey woolsey, but the unbleached, uncoloured material which is woven for all kinds of household use, or piece-dyed for men's wear, is quite a different thing. In its undyed state it is of a warm ivory tint, which makes a beautiful ground for printing, and in my first acquaintance with it, which was made through the women commissioners from Kentucky, Tennessee and Georgia during the Columbian Exposition, I made some most interesting experiments in block printing upon this natural background.

One can hardly expect that linsey woolsey will come into frequent or common use as a printed textile, since the two processes of hand-weaving and block-printing are not natural neighbours, but this capacity for taking and holding stains is of great value in embroidery, since it enables an artistic embroiderer to produce excellent effects with comparatively little labour. A clever needlewoman, working upon a fabric which takes kindly to stains, can apply colour in many large spaces and inter-spaces in her design which would otherwise have to be covered with stitchery, and in this way—which is a perfectly accepted and legitimate one—she gains an effect which would otherwise be costly and laborious.

From the composite nature of this domestic fabric, its cross-weaving of animal and vegetable fibre, it takes colour irregularly. Every cross-thread of wool is deeper in tone than the cotton thread it crosses, and this gives the quality which artists call vivacity or vibration. Linsey woolsey even when "piece-dyed" has something of this effect, and judicious and artistic colour treatment would complete its claims to be considered an art textile.

It is not to be supposed that the weavers themselves can work out this problem. It will need the direction and encouragement of educated and artistic women. Taking the fabric just as it exists, it is ready for the finer domestic processes learned by the women of the South during the hard years of the Civil War. The clever expedients of stitchery, the ways in which they varied their simple home-manufactures, and above all the knowledge gained of domestic "colouring," will be of inestimable value in the direction of artistic industries. In truth, Southern women have ways of staining and dyeing and producing beautiful colour quite unknown to other American women. They know how to get different grays and purples and black from logwood, and golden and dark brown from walnut bark, and all the shades of blue possible to indigo; and yellow-reds from madder, and rose-red and crimson from pokeberry, and one yellow from pumpkin and another from goldenrod; and they are clever enough to find mordants for all these dyes and stains, and make them indelible. It needs exactly the conjunction which we find in the South, of facile home-weaving, knowledge and practice of experimental dyeing, and love of practical art, to develop true art fabrics.

To show what linsey woolsey is capable of, I will instance a material woven in India in thin woolen strips of about twelve inches in width. It is what we should call a *sleazy* material to begin with. The strips of different colours are sewn, and very badly sewn, together, and they are also badly woven. Too flimsy for actual wear, they are simply admirable vehicles for colour, and to this quality alone they owe their popularity and importance. After being sewn together, the strips are generally embroidered in a rough way, with a constantly repeating figure on each breadth. The colour is certainly beautiful, a contrast of soft blues, and a selection of unapproachable browns—yellow-browns, red-browns, green-browns and gold-browns, with yellows of all shades, and whites of all tints, and this colour-beauty gives them a place as portieres and curtains where they do not belong by intrinsic or constitutional worth.

If one was intent only upon producing an imitation of the Bagdad curtains in linsey woolsey, it would be easy to weave narrow lengths of various colours, and by choosing those which were good contrasts or harmonies, and embroidering them together with buttonhole-stitch, or cat-stitch, or any ornamental stitch, to get something very like them in effect and far better in quality. But it should be the aim of domestic manufacture to do something which is *distinctive*, and therefore it would be better to start with the intention of producing the effect in one's own way. This could be done by weaving the cloth in full width (which should, if possible, be four feet), depending entirely upon the warp threads for colour. This, it may be remembered, is already one of the means of variation applied to linsey woolsey in weaving homespun dress goods; but in this case it must be carefully chosen art-effort, using colours which are in themselves beautiful. In depending upon the warp alone for colour the fact must be kept in mind that it will be much obscured by the over-weaving of the wool filling. It will be necessary, therefore, to use far stronger colours than if they were to stand unmixed or unobscured. Vivid blue, strong orange, flaming red and gold-brown could be used in the warp in stripes of about ten inches in width, with two inches of dead black on the sides and between each colour. The filling must be of one pale tint, either an ivory white or lemon yellow, or a very pale spring green woven over all. This would modify the violence of colour, giving an effect like hoar frost over autumn leaves. As a simple weaving this would have a beautiful effect, but when a coarse orange-coloured silk embroidery, consisting of a waved stem and alternate leaves, is carried down the centre of each black stripe, the simple length of linsey woolsey is transformed into what would be called a very Eastern-looking and valuable embroidery.

This is just one of its possible and easily possible adaptations for portieres and hangings. Quite another and perhaps equally popular one would be cross-colour upon a tinted warp. In this case the warp might be ivory white, yellow, light green, or even for darker effects, claret red, dark blue, dark green, or black. If an ivory white or light warp colour should be chosen, the cross-colours must be selected with special reference to the warp tint. A beautiful effect for a light room would be made on an ivory-coloured warp by weaving at the top and also below the middle a series of narrow stripes like a Roman scarf. There should be a finger's depth of rose colour at the top, and this would be obtained by a filling of light red, woven upon the ivory white warp. Then should come an inch stripe of pale blue, an inch of gold, another inch of blue; three inches of orange, then the inch of blue, the gold, and the blue again, and after that the rose-red for two-thirds the length of the portiere, when the ribbon stripes should again occur, after which the remaining third should be woven with a deeper red or a pale green.

Such a portiere would not require embroidery to complete its effect, for if the tints were pure as well as delicate, it would be a lovely piece of colour in itself.

This variety or style of hanging would have the advantage of throwing the burden of colour upon the wool, and as the animal fibre is apt to be more tenacious in its hold upon colour than vegetable, the question of fading would not have to be considered.

These two varieties of artistic homespun can by experiment be made to cover a great deal that is beautiful and artistic in manufacture, and yet it leaves untouched the extensive field of plain piece-dyed or yarn-dyed weavings. Yarn-dyed material always has the advantage of the possible use of two colours, one in the warp and one in the filling, but in certain places, as in upholstery, a solid colour produced by piece-dyeing would be preferable. Linsey woolsey dyed in fast and attractive colour would undoubtedly be a good material for upholstery of simple furniture, because of its strength and durability, but it seems to me its chief mission and probable future is to supply an exceptional art textile; one which has the firmness and flexibility belonging to hand-woven stuffs, and can be at the same time beautiful in colour, capable of hard wear and reasonably inexpensive. I am tempted to modify the last qualification, because no hand-woven goods ought to be or can be inexpensive, in comparison with those manufactured under every condition of competitive economy. And in truth, domestic weavings are sure of their market at paying prices, simply because they are what they are, *hand products*.

I have shown in a limited way some of the possibilities of artistic hand-weaving without touching upon cotton or flax diapers and damasks, since these cannot readily compete with power-weavings, but I have not spoken of the difference it would make in the lives of the mountain weavers of the South if their horizon could be widened by the introduction of art industries. Only those who know the joy and compensation of producing things of beauty can realize the change it might work in lives which have been for generations narrowed to merely physical wants; but there are many gifted Southern women who do fully realize it, and we may safely leave to them the introduction and encouragement of art in domestic manufactures.

NEIGHBOURHOOD INDUSTRIES

AFTER-WORD

I am often asked by women who are interested in domestic manufactures, how one should go to work to build up a profitable neighbourhood industry. To do this one must know the place and people, for anxious as most country women are to earn something outside of farm profits, they are both timid and cautious, and will not follow advice from unpractical people or from strangers.

In every farming community there will be one or two ingenious or ambitious women who do something which is not general, and which they would gladly turn to account. One woman may be a skilled knitter of tidies, or laces, or rag mats; another may pull rags through burlap, and so construct a thick and rather luxurious-looking door-mat; another may have an old-fashioned loom and weave carpets for all the neighbourhood; and each one of these simple arts is a foundation upon which an industry may be built, important to the neighbourhood, and in the aggregate to the country.

The city woman or club woman who wishes to become a link between these things and a purchaser must begin by improving or adapting them. She must show the knitter of tidies an imported golf stocking with all of the latest stitches and stripes and fads, and if the yarn can be had, undoubtedly the tidy-knitter can make exactly such another. When a good pair has been produced, the city friend will not have to look far among her town acquaintances for a "golf fiend," even if she herself is not one, and to him or her she must show the stocking and expatiate upon its merits: That it is not machine-made, but hand-knit; that it is thicker, softer, made of better material than woven ones, and above all, not to be found in any shop, but must be ordered from a particular woman who is a phenomenal knitter. All of which will be true, and equally so when the demand has increased and it has become a neighbourhood industry.

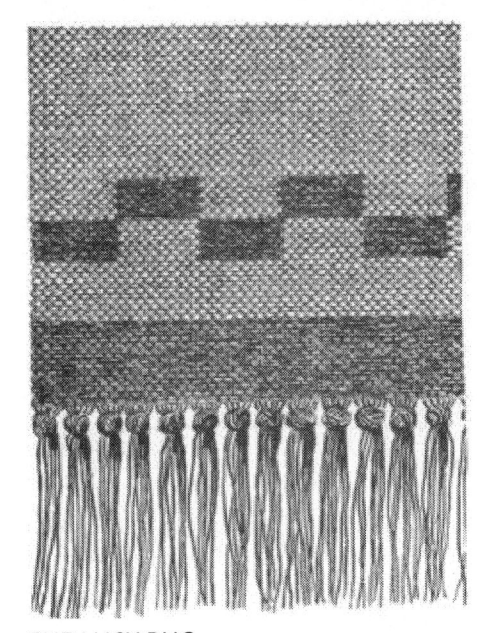

THE LUCY RUG

A golf player hardly need be told how to create a demand for hand-knit stockings, or how to assist the knitter by advice, both in the improvement and disposal of her wares; but it should be a veritable golf player and not a philanthropic amateur.

It is the same with other industries. The adviser must study them, improve them, adapt them, and find the first market, after which they will sell upon their own merits.

As far as I know, nothing has been done in the way of improvement of knitted mats or rugs, although a very beautiful manufacture has been founded upon the method of pulling rags through burlap. Knitted rugs have much to recommend them. They can be made of all sorts of pieces, even the smallest; they wear well, and can easily be made beautiful.

The building up of a rag carpet or rag rug industry is a much simpler matter, because the demand exists everywhere for cheap, durable and well-coloured floor covering. In my own experience I have found that the thing chiefly necessary is to teach the weavers that the colour must be pleasing and permanent, and to put them in communication with sources of supply of rags and warp. The rugs sell themselves, and probably will continue to do so.

The thing to remember when one wishes to be of use to their own and other communities, is that they must be sure of a commercial basis for the products before they encourage more than one person to begin a manufacture, and that the demand must be in advance of a full supply. Kindly and cultivated women who wish to be of real use to their summer neighbours will find this a true mission. Their lives lie within the current of demand, while the country woman lives within that of supply, and it is much easier for the city woman to bridge the space between than for her working neighbour. All good and well-founded industries take care of themselves in time, but until the merchant finds them out, and interposes the wedge of personal profit between things and their market—inciting and encouraging both—it seems to be the business of women in every lot of life to help each other.

Printed in Great Britain
by Amazon